Little Cub

For John

  —with love from Old Bear

Little Cub

Olivier Dunrea

Philomel Books
An Imprint of Penguin Group (USA) Inc.

A little cub lived all alone near the forest.

He did not like being alone.

He did not like the dark nights.

There was no one to take care of him.

Old Bear lived all alone deep in the forest.

He did not like being alone.

He did not like the dark nights.

There was no one to take care of him.

Every morning, the little cub splashed in the stream.

He watched the silvery fish swimming around his toes.

"Hmmpf," said the little cub. "I wish I knew how to catch a fish."

But there was no one to teach him.

Every morning, Old Bear trudged to the stream.

He caught a large fish for his breakfast.

"Hmmpf," said Old Bear. "I wish I had someone
to share this fish with."

But there was no one.

Every afternoon, the little cub scampered in the
meadow and looked for berries.
What he most longed for was the sweet honey
he could smell in the beehive in the hollow of a tree.
But the little cub was afraid of being stung by the bees.
His stomach was empty.
The little cub was often hungry.

Every afternoon, Old Bear ate a big lunch of oat cakes
spread thick with honey.
After eating his fill, he stretched out in the meadow
and took a nap.
His stomach was full.
Old Bear wasn't often hungry.

Every evening, the little cub curled himself
into a ball and tried to sleep.
He snuffled and whimpered.
He did not like to be alone at night.

Every evening, Old Bear trudged through the
tall grass to his cabin deep in the forest.
Old Bear grumbled and grumped.
He did not like to be alone all the time.
Being alone made him grumbly and grumpy.

One day, Old Bear heard a strange noise
coming from a pile of rocks.
He stopped and listened.
Old Bear peered into the rocks and saw a
little cub, curled into a ball, snuffling and kicking
in his sleep.

Old Bear leaned over the little cub and sniffed.

The little cub opened his eyes and yowled.

"Stop that yowling," said Old Bear.

And the little cub stopped yowling.

He stared at the big bear watching him.

"Who are you?" asked the little cub.

"I'm Old Bear," said Old Bear. "Who are you?"

"I'm me," said the little cub.

Old Bear and the little cub stared hard
at each other.

Neither of them blinked.

"Hmmpf," said Old Bear.

"Hmmpf," said the little cub.

Old Bear picked up the little cub.

"Who do you belong to?" asked Old Bear.

"I belong to me," said the little cub. "But maybe
I could belong to you."

Old Bear cradled the little cub.

The little cub felt safe in the big bear's arms.

He yawned loudly.

"I'm going to call you Little Cub," said Old Bear.

"I like that," said Little Cub.

Old Bear carried Little Cub to his cabin.

He gently placed Little Cub in the big bed.

He tucked the warm blanket around him.

"Will you teach me how to fish?" asked Little Cub.

"Yes, I will teach you how to fish. Now go to sleep,"
said Old Bear.

"Will you teach me how to get honey?"
asked Little Cub.

"Yes, I will teach you how to get honey. Now
go to sleep," said Old Bear.

"But I don't want to get stung by the bees,"
said Little Cub.

"I won't let you get stung by the bees,"
said Old Bear. "Now go to sleep."

Old Bear sat beside the bed.

Little Cub stared at Old Bear.

"What now?" asked Old Bear.

"I can't sleep," said Little Cub.

"Do you want me to tell you a story?"
asked Old Bear.

"Yes, I'd like that!" said Little Cub.

"I've never had a story before."

"Once upon a time, there was a grumpy old bear who lived all alone, deep in the forest . . . ," said Old Bear.

Little Cub closed his eyes.

He fell fast asleep.

He was no longer hungry.

He was no longer alone.

Old Bear sat by Little Cub all night long.

"Good night, Little Cub," said Old Bear.

"I'm glad you're here."

PHILOMEL BOOKS • A division of Penguin Young Readers Group.
Published by The Penguin Group. Penguin Group (USA) Inc., 375 Hudson Street, New York, NY 10014, U.S.A.
Penguin Group (Canada), 90 Eglinton Avenue East, Suite 700, Toronto, Ontario M4P 2Y3, Canada (a division of Pearson Penguin Canada Inc.). Penguin Books Ltd, 80 Strand, London
WC2R 0RL, England. Penguin Ireland, 25 St. Stephen's Green, Dublin 2, Ireland (a division of Penguin Books Ltd). Penguin Group (Australia), 250 Camberwell Road, Camberwell,
Victoria 3124, Australia (a division of Pearson Australia Group Pty Ltd). Penguin Books India Pvt Ltd, 11 Community Centre, Panchsheel Park, New Delhi - 110 017, India.
Penguin Group (NZ), 67 Apollo Drive, Rosedale, Auckland 0632, New Zealand (a division of Pearson New Zealand Ltd). Penguin Books (South Africa) (Pty) Ltd, 181 Jan Smuts Avenue,
Parktown North, South Africa 2193. Penguin Books Ltd, Registered Offices: 80 Strand, London WC2R 0RL, England.

Edited by Jill Santopolo. Design by Semadar Megged. Text set in 18-point Zapf Humanist 601 BT.
The artwork is rendered in pencil and gouache on 140 lb. d'Arches rough watercolor paper.
Library of Congress Cataloging-in-Publication Data is available upon request.

ISBN 978-0-399-24235-9
1 3 5 7 9 10 8 6 4 2

ALWAYS LEARNING   **PEARSON**